HOLLY'S FATHER REFUSED to look at her. He glared at the sidewalk instead, at the sky, at pairs of strangers sliding out of minivans and sprinting to the airport's entrance.

"You're hers if you get on that plane," he said. For weeks he'd been saying this. His skin had become sallow. The day before, Holly found clumps of his fine black hair stuck to shower walls.

"I know," Holly said. They'd first had this conversation on the day he decided to show her the postcard, and the week after, while he watched her purchase the plane ticket. It had hurt Holly then. And it hurt her now, being spoken to as some sort of possession making the wrong choice.

"Money's going to be tight."

"I know."

"But you're not going to call me."

"I know."

"Because you're not mine anymore."

"I know."

"If you do find her," Holly's father said, then reached into the bed of his blue Ford pickup, pulling a grey duffel bag from beneath a tarp he'd hooked taut, "I want you to tell her how much of a whore she is. I want you to tell her what I've become, what she's turned me into." He handed the bag over to Holly. It was light, a few pounds at most in the middle, weightless ends curved in the shape of a banana. "I didn't treat that woman right. I didn't at all. But what she did was unforgivable." He cleared his throat. "Can you do that for me?"

"Sure, Dad," Holly said. Lip service.

"And I want you to give her what's inside of that bag."

Holly pictured some sharp object in the bag, a butcher's knife, a piece of glass, something symbolic of how her father now felt, had been feeling. She then pictured herself going through security, being tackled, being detained, imprisoned, stuck in Arizona for the rest of her life, sent back to Wickenburg, sent back to him, to moments just like this. After carefully setting the duffel bag on the sidewalk, Holly leaned down to unzip the main pocket.

"There's a porcelain plate, two pairs of earrings and a picture frame. All of it's wrapped in layers of tissue paper." He waited for Holly to discover this for herself, then: "The things of hers I couldn't toss."

When Holly looked up at her father, when she saw just how hard he was biting his lip, she understood that the anger was only a mask, could only be a mask, and that he was horrible at wearing it. Seventeen years of discontent were torqued between every wrinkle that had formed on his face by age forty-one. And, what had evolved beneath those wrinkles, somewhere deep, Holly knew, was envy. Not just of Holly's mother, for the life she left him for, but of Holly herself. His daughter was leaving. No longer would she have to live in that peanut shell of a home, that love-cursed rambler from which, until now, there seemed no escape. No longer would she have to take long, aimless walks just to feel sane. No longer would she too have to deal with his pain—Hungry Man Thanksgivings on TV trays, weekends spent beer-buzzed, a lawn mown irregularly, when either Holly or her father couldn't hold out for the other any longer and caved. It was his now, all his, only his.

Holly hugged him then, tight. Tighter yet, her tanned face against the Winsol-scented chest of his khaki jacket. If this were it, if this were really it, if he were really disowning her, Holly would miss him. Not his pain; him. His uneven sideburns, the sharp angle of his nose. She'd miss the smell of Simple Green on his hands.

"Dad?"

"Yeah?"

"Am I doing the right thing?"

"You don't get to ask me that anymore."

###

November 14, 2012

Dear Holly,

The last time I saw you, you were just learning to walk. You won't remember this but I used to hold your left hand while you tried to take your steps. Your father held your right and together we'd all inch across the living room. I've been thinking about that a lot lately. Some days I can still feel those little fingers of yours in mine and I can't help but yield to the wave of regret that comes after. And I guess the only thing that I really need to say is that I'm sorry. It's the only thing to say. I'm sorry, Holly. I'm sorry that I left you, that I left when I did. I should've waited until you were older. I should've tried harder. I should've had the courage to come back. I'm sorry. I'd love to meet the grown you so I can hear about all the steps you've taken between then and now. If you at all feel the same way, you're more than welcome in Seattle.

Love,
Kaori

Orange cabs, yellow cabs, white cabs, cabs parking, squealing to the airport's curb, parking, squealing away, in and out like blackhawks evacuating soldiers from a battlefield. One of the orange cabs slammed to a halt in front of Holly. The passenger window was already down, a black man with a thin silver moustache in the driver's seat. "Where you need to be, sweetheart?" he asked with an East African accent.

Holly, after setting the duffel bag and her backpack on the back seat, pulled from her jacket pocket the slip of paper she'd written the address on. "The Freeman Building," she said, afraid she was somehow saying it wrong and, in case she was, providing further clarification, "it's on Cherry Street."

"I'll get you there," the driver said. He tilted the meter toward him, started it, then took off, smiling at Holly's insecurity. "You just relax. Enjoy the ride."

Holly looked at the car's clock. 4:16pm. The Freeman Building's leasing office closed at 5:00pm. She'd digitally signed her lease, and had digitally paid her security deposit. She would've paid her first month of rent that way, too, if she'd had the money then. But, she hadn't, and so she still had to hand her rent check over in order to get the keys to her apartment.

They tailgated the cabs in front of them until they were out of the airport's reach and on the highway. The highway took them over streets dotted with lean evergreens and past vehicles sporting bumper stickers that said, I'M KIND OF A BIG DEAL IN SEATTLE, or showed the cityscape in the shape of an umbrella.

"Does it really rain that much here?" Holly asked. The sky was dark, nearly dusk dark. Somewhere behind all of the slate grey clouds the sun was setting. But it wasn't raining, as she'd been led to believe it did in Seattle, every day. Her father had pointed that out at every opportunity, going so far as to say, "Seattle is the suicide capital of the U.S., you know." Which, following some Google research, she found was untrue. That title belonged to Las Vegas, followed by Colorado Springs and Tucson.

The driver chuckled. "It is January so yes, it will rain more. It's light rain, though, hardly any heavy rain."

"That's the only kind of rain where I'm from."

"From where I am, too." The driver looked in the rearview mirror and smiled. His teeth were the color of sand.

Though she figured he'd welcome the discussion, Holly opted not to bring up Wickenburg. She would not speak of it with pride—the newish library, the dude ranches, the mine. She would not lie and tell him he should visit someday, a mere saloon door to Phoenix. Yet, other than the three times she'd read over her mother's postcard, her hometown had been all she could think about on the flight. Her father. Graduation day. Sneaking onto golf courses at night with Sam, her lover at sixteen, and slitting garden hoses with box cutters.

The driver wiggled into a minor traffic jam on the interstate. Elevated as they were, Holly could see what she knew from online maps to be Puget Sound. Fog over the sea hindered her view of what lay on the other side, what exactly the ferry boats were sneaking toward, looking so small, like toys in a bathtub.

Holly looked at the car's clock. 4:31pm. She wanted to speak up, to let the driver know that there was no other option, that she had to be there by 5:00pm. But she hesitated, not knowing if that was impolite, being so demanding, so uncompromising when clearly there were factors at play out of the driver's control. At least we're still moving, Holly thought.

"So what brings you here, sweetheart?" the driver asked.

There it was. She'd been anticipating that question, dreading it, unable to settle on a surefire response. Three truths had brought her here, to Seattle, to this cab, to this traffic jam. Three truths she knew would inevitably lead to more questions from the driver, but also from anyone with whom she chose to disclose them.

TRUTH #1:
I came here to find my mother.

OUTCOMES (Q & A):
What's she like?
I don't know. She left before my 2nd birthday.

What does she do here?
She could be doing anything.

Where does she live?
My father Sharpied the address on the postcard.

TRUTH #2:
I came here to escape my father.

OUTCOMES (Q & A):
Escape?
He's all I've ever known.

Did he hurt you?
Yes, but not in the ways you're wondering.

What does he do?
Washes windows. Pouts. Repeat.

TRUTH #3:
I came here to find myself.

OUTCOMES (Q & A):
You don't know yourself?
Not at all.

What do you do?
Dream.

About what?
Not feeling alone.

"I need to do something new with my life," Holly eventually said. Something encompassing the three but with enough wiggle room to sidestep specifics in the questions that would ensue. Specifics like those, Holly thought, weren't for strangers; they were for the Sams of the world; they were for mothers.

"You seem young for a middle life crisis, sweetheart," the driver said. The traffic jam eased into motion within seconds, a white-gloved police officer waving vehicles around a rolled silver Impala. "How old are you?"

"Nineteen."

"No, no, no, too young. Much too young." They were back up to seventy-plus miles per hour now, passing vans struggling to shift from second to third, approaching overpasses on the outskirts of downtown. Skyscrapers came into view, and stadiums, and buses. "Nineteen is not for worries like that. Nineteen is for having fun, for dancing, for singing, for making money and kissing boys." He took the next exit, which looped west, toward Puget Sound. "You know what I mean, sweetheart?"

Holly didn't. She'd never understood why people discuss youth as if it were something to be tossed around lightly, as if choices at ten, or twelve, or nineteen do not have consequences. Choices of impact, Holly believed, could be made at any age. A life of meaning didn't have to start after a childhood of jackassery. Holly hated the wide margin of error given to children and teens and young adults. She saw it as farcical, even, the way young people were on one hand encouraged to live it up and make mistakes, and, on the other hand, expected to be better than anyone that had existed before them—farcical, and sad, the set up for failure. There remained a part of Holly, however, that worried the true fuel of this discontent was jealousy—that her margin of error had been far narrower, that her depressed father had hardly encouraged her to do anything, especially to make mistakes.

Holly didn't see the point in arguing with the driver, though. Relax, the driver had even said himself. And she wanted to try. Point A to Point B, she thought. "I understand," she said, then let silence sprawl its tense wings from window to window.

The next five minutes went on with the cab climbing and descending sloped streets while Holly, cheek pressed to the window, attempted to take in street names. Yesler and Spruce, Boren, Fir, and Alder. She gawked at monuments, at the skyscrapers, considering the care that had to have been taken in constructing such things. She pictured wrecking balls and cranes and high school graduates tiptoeing high beams, shaping the skeletons of these buildings with hammers and torches.

Then there were the faces. Attractive faces on bicycles, beaten faces dragging worn soles, wide eyes, narrow eyes, angled eyes. Black, white, tan, phantom-like, translucent. Faces beneath turbans, beneath bandanas and poet caps, above scarves and neckties and herringbone coats, homeless faces resting on cardboard stories. Diversity lived here, Holly had told herself while still in Wickenburg, and now saw with her own eyes. Mobility lived here. Resurgence was possible here.

They eventually double-parked on a west-facing down slope. Ahead, through a narrow break in the fog, Holly spotted mountains her aisle seat had prevented her from seeing on her descent. Not the rounded mounds of soft rock and clay she and Sam had hiked over in Arizona, but mountains. Upwards of 5,000 feet. Real mountains, travel guide mountains, snowcaps. She pictured her apartment high enough to breathe them in as she woke.

"Which one is the Freeman Building?" Holly asked. Each immediate building looked the same to her: short, narrow and bricked either red or yellow.

The driver pointed to the south side of the street, at a yellow building with a short staircase and a glass door. He tilted the meter toward her. "$47.50, sweetheart.

Holly's stomach split, the bottom half sinking, the top half stretching to her throat like wet dough. Idiot, she thought, you fucking hick idiot. Quickly she reached into her backpack and pulled out her wallet. Thirty dollars. A few quarters, some pennies. Her father had given her an extra $15 to check the duffel bag he'd given her, but $15 hadn't covered it and Holly had had to dip into her own cash.

"Sir," Holly said. She cleared her throat. "Sir, I only have thirty dollars."

The driver rubbed his face as if he'd been expecting that response, as if he'd bypassed anger altogether and only disappointment remained, not in her, but in himself, in having laid the groundwork for the acceptance of mistakes. He reached over into the passenger seat and shifted loose papers around, as well as a stack of paperbacks from the library, searching for his credit card reader. No luck. He moved his travel mug out of the cup holder and searched there but, still, nothing. Not in the glove compartment or the center console either. He sighed. "Let's go to the ATM then."

Holly looked at the car's clock again. 4:48pm. If they searched for an ATM, she could miss getting into the Freeman Building entirely. She could be on the street for the night, or at a hotel whose nightly fee would gouge what little money she'd saved. "I don't have any time to go to an ATM," Holly said. "I'm so sorry. I know you don't have any proof, but please believe me when I say I'm good for it. I'll be here for six months—that's how long my lease is. At least six months. I'll be right here, sir, in this building. I'll see you again."

"This is a big city, sweetheart."

"I know, but—but come back tomorrow even and I'll be able to pay you the difference." Now, more than she had in the past five hours, Holly wished she'd begged her father for his truck. Hands and knees begged, I'll-call-her-a-whore-as-many-times-as-you-want-me-to begged.

"Wait," Holly said, brightly. "I have checks, I can pay you with a check—"

"I don't accept checks."

"Do you have a business card then? Here, give me your business card and I'll call you."

"I don't have a business card." The cab driver sighed. "Why didn't you just take the light rail?"

Holly had no clue what the light rail was. She'd never heard of such a thing. Fucking hick. Tears came on, confused tears, panicked tears, soundless tears that, had he not looked in the rearview mirror, the driver never would've noticed.

"Don't cry, sweetheart," he said. "Please, don't cry. You need the money for food, yes? And for a toothbrush and such?"

Holly nodded while wiping her eyes.

"Now you know how much it costs to take a cab. Correct?" He waited for Holly to nod, then said, "Public transit is good here. Best option if you're on a tight budget." And finally, as he cleared the meter, more to himself than to Holly: "Consider your first cab ride in Seattle my gift to you and your new life."

###

Holly slid her inflated air mattress across the hardwood floor and against the wall, its plastic lining sounding to her like a cat sharpening its claws. There were deep gouges on the hardwood, assumedly from previous tenants dragging recliners and sofas and tables and ottomans, from one corner to another. 265 square feet in all, one bathroom just barely larger than a bookcase, a lone east-facing window in the kitchenette that glimpsed some cluttered apartment across the alley with a vase of wilted roses on the windowsill. Though each eggshell wall was dry to the touch, they, as if the maintenance crew had turned the apartment that morning, smelled of fresh paint.

Holly knew that she shouldn't like the space. She knew that she shouldn't look at it and think to herself that the $850 check written upon arrival was well spent. It was run-down. There were water spots on the ceiling shaped like dead tree branches. Each light bulb gave off a different tint, dim yellow to near-blinding white and back to yellow. But the place was hers. Hers. Hers!

Much could be done to make 265 square feet unique, she thought. Matching black leather furniture, glass tables, bright red rugs. As she'd been picturing since Sam, her first apartment would be made modern. Clean, straight lines. Sleek. Little, if anything, on the walls—framed aerial photographs of Arizona, successive as if telling a story of her journey, her roots. But that was all. Because this wouldn't be a place to dwell on the past. No they'd think of the future here. This wouldn't be a place to sit for hours on end and binge TV shows, but a place for she and her mother and her friends to breathe, to recuperate after hiking those western mountains, to prepare for a night out in gorgeous dresses, sipping from stemmed wine glasses.

Soon, Holly told herself. Soon enough, that day would come. First, she had to get a job. And on days off from that job, she'd use time and money to find her mother. She'd go beyond the fruitless Google searches, beyond the dollars and moments to be wasted on the most recent edition of the phone book. She didn't know how exactly she'd do it, but she'd find her mother. And everything else would follow.

Soon, she reminded herself. She then eased herself onto the air mattress and reached for her unzipped backpack, from which she pulled a laptop. Once open and running, Holly searched for available networks not requiring a password for access. BROCKER50791 was the only one without a chain icon. Holly clicked on it. Access granted.

Forget email, forget Facebook; she immediately went to Craigslist. seattle/tacoma > jobs > food/bev/hosp. Dozens of positions listed just that day. FT/PT servers, AM/PM cashiers, dishwashers, bartenders, bakers, bussers, baristas, barbacks, Beecher's Cheese cutters, so many words starting with a B, so many damn words in front of her, opportunities for her to smile at. She couldn't help but smile. She couldn't stop smiling. She'd spent five days in Wickenburg perfecting her résumé, drawing as much attention as possible to her three summers as "Busser/Server" at Harvey's BBQ, to that one full year as "Front Desk Clerk" at the Scorpion Tail Inn. Snagging a 'getting-by' position, Holly felt, was going to be easier than she'd initially thought. She had references, good references. For God's sake, she had Harvey Preen III himself to attest for her punctuality, her willingness to learn, her communication skills. He'd said it himself the day she told him she needed to work full-time, year round, that she was taking the job at Scorpion Tail: "We're going to miss you, Holly."

###

In the same clothes she'd worn the day before—denim jacket and tight black jeans—Holly walked across Cherry St. toward her apartment building, clutching one paper bag filled with items she'd been too busy to buy before nearby stores closed: a throw pillow, a blanket, toothbrush, toothpaste, deodorant, shampoo, toilet paper, a shower curtain, a day-old (and half-off) baguette she planned to gnaw on throughout the day. In her other hand was the folded cash she'd just withdrawn from the 7/11's ATM; she'd taken out $40 that she planned to stick in an envelope marked DRIVER—THANK YOU, along with fifteen dollars she'd already had. She didn't know if, or when, she'd see him again. But if she did, it was important to her to be ready. It was important to her to properly say thank you. She stuffed the cash into her pants pocket as she continued walking.

Last night, Holly had slept for maybe two hours. Tossed and turned, either too cold, too excited, or too foreign to the noises blanketing her in the night. Sirens, car alarms, an offbeat drip/drizzle sonata in her tub, drunken shouting down on the street. From the apartment above her, no later than 6:00am: the pitter-patter of a small dog's paws, the vibration of a treadmill at walking speed. None of it had angered Holly. Not even as she stared down a distorted version of herself in her building's glass door. Her hair was greasy and matted. Her clothes were wrinkled, skin and lips dry but not yet cracking. She scratched plaque from her front teeth and wiped it on her jeans, then unlocked the door with her key, anxious to be free of the filth she'd allowed to form.

Holly saw that Michelle's office door was open. Some bass-heavy techno track from her computer's speakers overpowered the ringing of her work phone. The few times she'd spoken to Michelle on that phone had led Holly to believe that Michelle was pushing forty. Her voice was deep, calm, soothing, a slight rasp at the end of each word that Holly felt hinted at jazz clubs, at Boulevardiers, and escapades. Which is why it had surprised Holly the day before to see that

Michelle was nowhere near forty, but closer to twenty-five. She had long legs and kiwi green eyes, short black hair and the cutest freckles strung across her cheeks like bistro lights. Michelle was Sam; Sam, with more lines on her face, and slightly darker lips. Sam, with smaller ears but just as much soul. Michelle was beautiful. Holly had never felt right walking away from beautiful.

Michelle sat behind her chaotic desk, finding elbow room somewhere between staplers and sticky notes, her head propped by a flat palm. The phone kept ringing. One ring, two rings, three. Michelle seemed to reach for the phone, though the movement turned out to be a mere stretching of a kinked wrist. It took her a moment to spot Holly and, when she did, it took one more moment for her to a) turn her music down and b) remember exactly whom Holly was.

"There's my newbie," Michelle said. "How was your first night?"

Holly clung to 'my newbie', imagined it as a cartoonish bubble growing out of Michelle's mouth, 'my' italicized. "Good," Holly said. Somehow, despite the reality of how it had been, Holly, in Michelle's presence, was convinced that this was the truth. "It was good."

"Sit, sit," Michelle said, waving Holly to one of two chairs in front of the desk. She had on black and white striped mittens, fingers buttoned back to the knuckles. Bad circulation. Whisper: Baby, I'm cold. "Finding everything okay? Having any trouble with the buses?"

"No trouble at all," Holly said. Which wasn't true. She hadn't taken a bus, hadn't spotted a stop that didn't house hard women with jagged teeth, or men scratching at their forearms and obliques, at scabs on their shins. Truth was, other than field trips, Holly had never stepped foot on a bus. Carpools. Bicycles. Walks. Her father would pick her up after work. He'd mumble about his day, chug what remained of the Sprite he'd been nursing, pull into the nearest gas station for a new case.

"I'm glad," Michelle said. "If you get a chance, you should head up to Ballard."

Ballard sounded familiar, as if it was a word Holly should've taken note of weeks ago, when researching Seattle, reading up on the neighborhoods of Queen Anne, and Wallingford, and Fremont, picturing her mother as either a businesswoman in a pantsuit living blocks from the Space Needle, or a woman in homemade overalls, sharing a commune in the treetops. Maybe her cab driver had mentioned Ballard. Her face apparently gave away her mind's pursuit.

"It's my favorite neighborhood," Michelle said. "Quaint, lots of cute little shops. There's this one coffee place, Penelope's. My friends are crazy about it."

"Are you crazy about it?"

The rasp carried over to her high-pitched laugh; a chickadee with a cigarette. "I mean, I like it. Yeah, I like it. Well, it's okay. I tend to spend more time at bars than I do at coffee shops." She gave Holly a look that said she knew saying such a thing was mischievous and it made Holly wonder if Michelle spoke to the rest of the tenants in the same way— even the elderly men and women Holly had seen stepping into the elevator on her floor—or if she was slick enough to adjust for all, for each age bracket. "There's one I go to often called The Viking's Head that I think would fit your vibe." Michelle wrote the name on a sticky note and handed it to Holly.

Which confused Holly. Michelle had seen Holly's driver's license. She'd made copies. Nineteen years of age was on file, somewhere, everywhere. Still, Holly thought, she was to burn no bridges, especially that extending to the striking woman across the desk she felt guilty both staring at and looking away from.

"I'll have to check it out," Holly said. "Thank you."

"You're very welcome. Seriously, if you need anything— a recommendation, directions, whatever—you know where to find me. I've gotten to know this city pretty well."

At this moment, Holly considered asking Michelle if she'd ever encountered a woman named Kaori Porter, or if there was anyone on her extensive contact list that had, someone to guide Holly toward one of the things for which she'd come to Seattle. But there'd be questions. Deep questions, and the deep would turn dim, and then dark, darker than Holly was willing to go with Michelle here and now. Broken, dislocated, irreparable: the last things she wanted this woman to think of her.

"Where are you from?" Holly eventually asked. She guessed California, then Florida, places Holly thought responsible for producing beauty.

"Indiana," Michelle said, and scrunched her face as if the word alone made her nauseous. "Don't even ask." She waited for Holly to finish laughing, then: "Lived with my brother for a while in the U District, at least until I could get on my feet. Do you have family here?"

Holly thought of her mother, of the postcard, of the family portrait she'd watched her father smash when she was five. How even then, with her baby daughter in her arms, her mother had looked unsure of herself, a crooked smile, that scar above her right eyebrow sloppily covered by makeup. She wanted to tell Michelle her mother's name. She wanted to tell Michelle stories she'd never been told, about her mother's Japanese heritage, about her mother's family, that they were pure, divine. But Michelle's phone rang once more, this time seemingly twice as loud as before.

"I'm sorry," Michelle said. "I should probably take this though."

"It's no problem," Holly said, and stood. "We'll talk soon." And they would. Holly would make sure they would.

A day later, the first response came. Fractured gray light bled through the kitchenette window. Holly sat cross-legged on her air mattress, holding her Pop-tart to the side, careful not to get crumbs on her keyboard.

Dear Holly,

Thank you for your interest in the position of Barista. Unfortunately, we have decided to move forward with the application process without you. We do, however, encourage you to apply to more positions through our esteemed company as they become available. Best of luck in your job search.

Another, near dark:

Dear Holly,

*Thank you for your interest in the position of Part-time
Server. Unfortunately, we have decided to move forward with the
application process without you.*

The next morning, two more responses came that said
the same exact thing: "Unfortunately, we have decided to
move forward with the application process without you."

Rattled wasn't the right word to describe how Holly felt.
Neither was confused, or furious, or defeated. Glum, maybe,
melancholic. Deflated, like a tire, like a balloon mistied and
released into a clear sky but now tumbling back to earth. She'd
been rejected before, but not like this, not this way, through
emails sent by strangers, complete strangers who'd glanced for
eight seconds at titles and bullet points and dragged her
documents to a digital folder labeled NO.

How much easier it was, Holly thought, to be denied by
those close to you. How much easier it was to have her father,
a man who had watched both her strengths and flaws evolve,
condemn her decision to fly to Seattle. How much simpler it
had been for Sam to take Holly's fingers out of her and walk
off of the sixth green—a par-three—into town, to Evan, who
she'd days later hold hands with down the hallway, eyes on her
knees, her gorgeous fucking knees.

Pathetic. That was the word. Pathetic, to the point of lying on her back all afternoon, in her underwear, on her air mattress, still the only piece of furniture in her studio. To the point of taking half an hour to listen to the tenant above take a shower, all the while watching the water stains on her ceiling grow toward one another, three branches with intentions of convergence. Pathetic to the point that, instead of searching for and applying to more jobs, all she could bring herself to view online was her bank account. $417.78. Groceries, the public transit card she'd loaded in order to avoid carrying so much coin.

She wanted to scroll through her contact list and call Sam and confess to her how pathetic she was for still thinking of her three years later, for still wanting her. She'd define the word for her, she'd explain its origins, she'd use it in five sentences for her if it provoked Sam to say some version of, "I'm sorry," in that timid voice, the S and long O shoving themselves through that twig-wide gap between her front teeth, "For leading you on, for making you chase."

And she wanted to call her father. With limited minutes, of course, he'd agreed to keep her flip phone on his plan. "For two months," he told her. "Two months is all I'll give you. After that, you're on your own."

But she thought maybe a call now would be worth it. It wouldn't matter which words he chose to use—"You are pathetic", "Fuck you"—or if he was drunk, or which tone the words rolled along. She wanted to hear his voice. She wanted to know if he was ready to tell her the truth about her mother. Not just, "She's a whore," or, "She didn't like us," or, "She's a whore that didn't like us," none of the vague, overused excuses, no more dodging, no more hiding, no more suppression.

"Did she really fuck other men?" Holly would ask him. "Did you beat her? Is that how she got that scar? Is that what drove her to Seattle? And why Seattle? Why didn't you say a goddamn word about Seattle? Why, Dad? And why would you cross out the address? I know why. You don't want me to find her because you know she'll tell me that you beat her into fucking other men. Isn't that right?" She pictured herself gasping for air, saying in under a minute what she hadn't ever been able to say to his face. "Or was she like me? Huh, Dad? Did she like women? Was she guilted into dating you, into marrying you, into making me? Huh, you persistent fuck? Huh? What makes a woman a whore?" He wouldn't say a word. She wouldn't let him. Because she'd have an epiphany, right there, phone pressed to her cheek. "You're pathetic. And you've made me pathetic.

Click.

She'd hang up. She'd feel euphoric, but filthy, as if she were atop an oceanfront dune, wind whipping sand into her hair and pores. She'd clean herself, and what then? Back to the air mattress? Back to sending out her résumé? Within an hour, within a day, within a week, all signs back to pathetic?

Best to conserve the minutes for phone interviews, Holly thought.

She rolled off of the air mattress and stood, conscious of but ignorant to the popping her stiff joints made. She hurried to the duffel bag she'd placed against the opposite wall, picked it up and walked into the bathroom. She sat on the toilet and unzipped the duffel. Bundled in one bulky, wretchedly-taped package were her mother's items. Holly tore into the tissue paper, hearing the pearl earrings roll across the surface of the plate. She'd never seen these things, hadn't known her father had hung onto something of her mother's. Where had he kept them? Under his bed? In his toolbox? Somewhere in his packrat closet?

Earrings in hand, where he'd hidden them no longer mattered; they were beautiful, even in the dim yellow light of her apartment. Two pair, one small, one much larger, gaudier, but both studs and with gold stems. Holly set the earrings gently on the kitchen counter and lifted out of the duffel her mother's porcelain plate.

Rectangular and with a white base, the plate's design was of a giant oak with a rope swing dangling beneath its thickest branch, a child swinging parallel to the ground. Intricate, Holly thought. Beautiful. Her mother was beautiful. Her mother was a beautiful creature, some beautiful creature her ugly father damaged. At first, she could barely stand to look at the framed photo beneath it all, the earrings and plate. It was a school picture of Holly, age eight, and so much of her was her father: those big hick ears, a miniature but angled hick nose, a thin hick mouth. Of her mother, she'd been given light tan skin, dark hair and eyes. And it still wasn't enough. Those missing teeth should've been her mother's. That faintest of scrapes on her chin from when she fell off of her bicycle should've been her mother's. If her mother had been there, she never would've worn that ugly Yosemite Sam sweater. She never would've sat before that photographer with frizzy hair. She never would've ended up here, in Seattle, not in this way, on a toilet seat and pathetic.

###

CL>seattle>for sale/wanted>jewelry
PEARL EARRINGS—GOOD QUALITY

Can sell them to you individually ($75 for the small, $100 for the larger), or as a set ($150). I'm no jewelry expert but, as you can see in the pictures, both sets of earrings are in good condition. If you'd like to see more pictures, just ask. If you're interested in buying, please respond. I'll be in touch shortly after that. Thanks, and have a great day!

-Holly

Immediately after opening the Freeman Building door, Holly heard a man yelling. Muffled but still vicious; a rabid dog with the cage door locked. She found herself gravitating toward the yelling, leaning an ear closer and closer to Michelle's office. At first, Holly thought that Michelle was gone for the day, sick or otherwise, her substitute taking himself too seriously over a conference call, or unable to control his emotions with a repeatedly destructive tenant. But then, briefly, there was her voice.

"Get your fucking hands off me, you fuck!"

Holly opened the door. Over Michelle's desk stood a thin white man with baggy gray chinos and a short, wide mohawk. He was young, younger than Michelle and, upon noticing Holly in the doorway, he took his hands from Michelle's wrists. He turned to Holly. His eyes were denim blue, and bloodshot. Michelle rolled her chair along the wood floor, away from him.

"Hey Holly," Michelle said, damp eyes communicating something of gratitude for the interruption. "Did maintenance look at those water stains yet?" She cleared her throat. "Did they?"

Holly had mentioned the stains to Michelle but hadn't formally submitted a maintenance request. This was an act. "Yeah," Holly said, walking closer to the desk, "yeah, they took a look at them." The man smelled of gasoline as he walked past her. There were dark stains on his light green jacket, flecks of white paint on the sleeves. He slammed the door behind him and only then did Holly ask Michelle: "Are you okay?"

"Oh, that?" Michelle said. Her eyes fluttered about—ceiling, desk, floor, wrist. She forced a smile. "That was nothing."

"Are you sure?" She considered saying something else, something more. That wasn't nothing. Considered pressing for information, for the identity of the man, for the basis of he and Michelle's relationship. Deterring him from violence, Holly felt, should result in such information. She deserved that. At least that. She wondered if he was an ex-lover, a former tenant, a former employee, even a friend who frequented Penelope's, someone Michelle had unintentionally crossed. Because Michelle would cross no one willingly. She couldn't. Look at her. Vulnerable looked even better on her than confident.

"What can I do for you, Holly?"

Something in the way Michelle asked that question signaled to Holly that playtime was over. She'd been looking at her black and white mittens. She'd said it slowly, and with gravel in her voice. As brief as it'd been, no longer would they sit in this office, or anywhere else, and flirt. It would be too embarrassing for Michelle. Holly had thrust herself into something she never should've seen, something Michelle probably never wanted her to see. And neither could go back.

"I was wondering if you had any postcards laying around." Which was true. If she couldn't call her father, she'd mail him, at the very least let him know where she can be reached.

"I think so," Michelle said. She walked to a trio of filing cabinets against the back wall and opened a drawer. Everything about her body language said she no longer cared. "Choose which one you'd like."

Holly walked over, looked in the drawer, chose the most generic one she could, with the Space Needle Warhol-ed on the front. She nodded her gratitude at Michelle and walked toward the door.

"Here," Michelle said, "You'll need a stamp." She ripped one from the book on her desk and handed it to Holly. The Liberty Bell, cracked.

"Thanks," Holly said.

"Look, Holly—"

"It's fine," Holly interrupted. "Just let me know if you need anything, okay." She knew Michelle wouldn't, that she'd swallow whatever it was, even teeth and blood, before further exposing her problems to this just-met transplant. Yet, Holly felt it needed to be said, and was pleased to have Michelle meet her words with a smile, fake as it was.

Dear Holly,

I'm interested in both pairs of earrings. I'd really like to get a look at them before I commit to $150 though. That's nothing against you. Just want to make sure they're right for daughter. I look forward to hearing from you.

Sincerely,
Zayra

Dear Holly,

Thank you for your interest in the position of Barback. Unfortunately, we have decided to move forward with the application process without you.

Dear Holly,

Thank you for your interest in the position of Administrative Assistant. Unfortunately, we have decided to move forward with the application process without you.

Dear Holly,

Thank you for your interest in the position of Courtesy Clerk. Unfortunately, we have decided to move forward with the application process without you.

Dear Zayra,

It was so nice to meet you and your daughter today! She's such a cutie and I'm so glad she liked the earrings. That's all I wanted to say, really. Please do let me know if you need any help at the art gallery. Would be more than happy to offer my services. Take care!

Sincerely,
Holly

Dear Holly,

Thank you for your interest in the position of Customer Service Representative. Unfortunately, we have decided to move forward with the application process without you.

Dear Holly,

Thank you for your interest in the position of Cleaning Assistant. Unfortunately, we have decided to move forward with the application process without you.

Dear Holly,

Thank you for your interest in the position of Sales Rep. Unfortunately, we have decided to move forward with the application process without you.

Dear Dad,

Hope all is well. Thought you might like to have my address on hand. So, there it is. Things are going great here. Meeting a lot of nice people, enjoying the scenery. Call me if you'd like.

Love,
Holly

Dear Holly,

It was so nice to meet you too! Isn't she precious!? Me and Vern can't get enough of her. As for the gallery... We aren't currently seeking help but that doesn't mean we can't work anything out in the future. Maybe in 2-3 months? That'd probably be the earliest. I'll talk to Vern about it sometime soon and get back to you. Sound good? Forgot to say this earlier: Welcome to Seattle!

> *Sincerely,*
> *Zayra*

CL>seattle>for sale/wanted>household items
FLAWLESS DESIGNER PLATE FOR SALE

> *One of a kind Japanese plate that has never been used. Has been passed down through my family for generations. $475 OBO. Needs to go soon. If you'd like to see more pictures, just ask.*

> *-Holly*

###

From her window seat on the 40 bus, Holly watched the sunlight burn through yet another grey morning. It seemed to turn Lake Union back to blue, what leaves remained on damp trees to green. Cyclists came out of hiding, weaving through traffic fast enough that their silver breaths trailed instead of led. The bus approached a stop in the Fremont neighborhood. Several on the bus stood, neck strained, eyes down at their phones, headphones on. They danced around one another in a somewhat orderly fashion toward the exits, which, considering how no one had said a word, Holly found remarkable. As they filed off, aboard came several more, occupied, eyes down, mouth shut. Replaced, not entirely unlike Michelle had been.

Giovanni Brenko, late thirties and with slicked brown hair, had been in Michelle's office chair for the past eight days. He smelled of chicken nuggets and Old Spice and had a thick nose and the wide-set eyes of a mustang, near oblivious of what stood before him unless he turned his head. He answered the phone on the first ring. He listened to The Carpenters, seemingly on repeat. He'd treated Holly as if she were twelve.

"Portland," Giovanni had said, and slowly, speaking of his roots. "It's a city in Oregon. Oregon isn't too far from here. It's a state along the Pacific Coast."

Empty-handed Holly stood in the leasing office, nodding, knowing within seconds of meeting him that there was nothing she could do to change the narrative: he'd always think she was this dumb.

"Is there anything else I can help you with?"

"Yeah." Holly paused then, maneuvering a way to ask what was on her mind without offending Giovanni. "Has Michelle been relocated to another property or—?

"Well," Giovanni said, crossing his arms, "I'm not at liberty to discuss that." He leaned back in Michelle's chair.

"And do you think you should be worrying about where she's gone?"

Holly shrugged. Bit the inside of her cheek to keep from thinking of how much she hated being spoken to like this. "I mean, she's a human, so yeah, I think it's okay to worry."

Holly had multiple times pictured that man strangling Michelle with a piece of rope in a dimly lit park, leaving her for a different man to find and defile. She pictured that man beating Michelle's temples with a book as thick as his thigh, then slamming it on her kidneys as she fell to the ground. Holly had even splurged days earlier and purchased a copy of the Seattle Times, relieved to not find a Michelle of any kind in the obituaries.

"Well," Giovanni said, visibly frustrated. "I assure you that Michelle is safe and healthy."

"Northwest Market Street," the bus's automated voice announced.

Holly tugged the cord above her. A ding sounded through the bus, registering her request. When the bus came to a complete stop, Holly, eyes open, ears uncovered, backpack tight on her shoulders, exited, then walked two and a half blocks west, where, there, on the north side of the street, stood Penelope's.

On one wall of the coffee shop hung a painting of an elephant with disproportionate tusks. On the opposite wall was a mural of some prairie, a blurred cheetah hunting a gazelle, a lion lying nearby, colorful birds overhead, some others perched on the lone tree in the center. Against each wall sat leaning customers, whispering customers, old customers, young customers. The aroma was aggressive, as if Holly had just jammed a slit coffee bean up each nostril.

A barista with the complexion of blond wood wiped the counter as she spoke to Holly: "You're gonna be glad you came in today." Her forearms were muscular, but not too muscular, defined, but not overtly so—strong and attractive as she gripped that cloth.

"Why's that?" Holly was at the counter now.

The barista held a smile that gave away just how happy she was Holly hadn't avoided her trap. "Well, today, and just for today, we're offering a reduced rate on what we call Tiger Fang. Have you ever heard of it?"

Holly hadn't, and said so.

Spot on, in rhythm, the barista said: "It's a dry-processed Ethiopian blend that you'll find has both citrus and floral accents. You'll also find hints of jasmine and cocoa, pineapple and rhubarb." The barista paused, either having forgotten what came next in her pitch, or trying to let her awkward yet confident silence do the rest of the selling. She eventually caved. "It's to die for," she said.

"It's really that good?"

"Babe, it's the best. Would you like to try a sample?"

Holly nodded, watched the barista release some Tiger Fang into a fluoride cup and bring it over. Babe. She'd never been called that, by anyone. Holly took a sip when the barista returned. She'd liked coffee since she was thirteen or fourteen, but had never loved it. Enough to not settle for instant coffee, but not enough to frequent coffee shops. And so she immediately questioned herself, her tastes, and her status when she thought the Tiger Fang was good, not great. She could taste a hint of citrus fruit—something acidic, at least— though she wouldn't classify it as pineapple. Otherwise, it tasted like coffee. Like really, really strong coffee. She took another sip.

"It's like sex, right?" the barista said. Whatever she did with her eyebrows—a raising of them, a lowering, what was it that she did?—hinted at Holly that she'd been having plenty of it.

Holly smiled. "I'll take a small cup."

"That's my girl," the barista said. She turned around, grabbed a clean eight-ounce coffee mug. "That'll be four dollars, babe."

Four dollars? Four dollars!?

The barista's smile, as well as her general air of friendliness, disappeared once the sale had been verbally made. Despite her internal objection, Holly handed over her four dollars and, Tiger Fang in hand, Holly walked to the middle of the coffee shop and sat at a table for two facing NW Market St. Four dollars. Four fucking dollars. Holly unzipped her backpack and pulled out her laptop. While the machine warmed, she watched squinting flannels walk past the front door, and peacoats, V-necks and beards and stocking caps. Some even wore sunglasses, their eyes anything but accustomed to the winter sunlight. After she connected her laptop to Penelope's WiFi, Holly logged in to her email account.

Dear Holly,

I am very much hoping your plate is still for sale. Even now, when I'm supposed to be working, I can't help but look at it and be transported back to my childhood. Such a gorgeous thing it is. I will say upfront that $470 does seem a little high for me. That doesn't mean that it doesn't have value, just that the highest I think I'd be able to go would be $425 or so. Would that work for you? Please do let me know. Talk to you soon.

Sincerely,
Donald Koh

Holly opened another tab and logged in to see her bank account. $471.46. She had two weeks before the month turned. The absolute lowest she could take and be able to pay for another month of rent was $379. Take the $425, Holly thought. You'll be able to cover the electric that way, too. You can do that. You can go two weeks without spending a dime. There are some crackers left. And a can of tuna. A few bites for each meal. You've got this.

Holly returned to Donald's email and hovered over the "Reply" button for a few seconds before clicking. She wondered if she could hold out any longer, if she'd be making a mistake by setting up a meet-and-greet. She wondered if somewhere out there her mother was scouring Craigslist for something totally unrelated to the plate, but somehow, somehow she soon would stumble upon the ad, see the picture, see it signed "Holly" and lose her breath, catch that lost breath, reply. Meet. Hug and cry, cry and hug, help Holly pay rent, help Holly find a job, offer Holly a place of comfort, solace, do her part in ending this struggle. But it was wrong. Holly knew it was wrong, to expect a miracle. Wrong to think that her mother would somehow find her, wrong to doubt, even for a second, that the only move she could make was to buy time.

Dear Donald,

Just then Holly was distracted by a pregnant woman with wet hair being pushed past the Penelope's entrance by a skinny man in a hooded sweatshirt. He was yelling at her as he did so. She was in tears. The whispers within the coffee shop ceased altogether, all eyes on the entrance, all asses in seats. Holly thought of Michelle. Holly thought of her mother, pictured a young, drunk version of her father angry about what would later be thought nothing, but shoving—just shoving, shoving-shoving-shoving Holly's mother across the sidewalk, into a building, into traffic. And then something in Holly's gut turned, churned, boiled, roiled, did something with just enough force, just enough power to stand her up and walk her past all of Penelope's seated onlookers, cup of Tiger Fang in hand.

"You can't take that cup outside," the barista said.

But Holly opened the door with her free hand. Out she walked, to the skinny man, who was now waiting to cross the street. She tapped him on the shoulder and, before he could turn entirely around, Holly flung her Tiger Fang all over the left side of his face. Steam rose from his cheeks. He howled, some hybrid of coyote and man, a howl that intensified as he pressed his fingers to the blotches. Holly hoped that it wouldn't end, that his burnt face would blister, that it would be gawked at by passersby, that his stubble would smell like coffee for days.

And then, her eyes still on the man, Holly was shoved to the side. Again. And again, until balance was lost.

"What the fuck, bitch?" the pregnant woman yelled at her. Her breath smelled like gin and Juicy Fruit gum. Tears would not stop falling from her eyelashes. She repeated it as she shoved, both her hands and her words gaining power: "What the fuck, bitch?"—shove—"What the fuck, bitch?"— shove. The only thing that deterred her from her pursuit of Holly was the groaning, coffee-covered man who had curled himself on the sidewalk, to whom she waddled to and said, "Baby, are you okay? Baby?"

Holly watched as the pregnant woman helped lift the skinny white man to his feet. They walked east on Market St. together, toward nothing but the same. He would beat her for this. In his eyes, it would be her fault. And maybe it was, Holly thought. Maybe she was in the wrong, staying with him, encouraging a lost cause to be a better man, birthing his child, something that would link them together for the rest of their existence.

Holly went back inside Penelope's, back to whispers. She returned the empty cup to the barista, then packed her things, exited, and stomped west on Market St, until she could go no further. Up 34th Ave. she went, north as the sky closed back into layer upon layer of gray, up steep inclines with no purpose other than to walk, just walk, until her lungs hurt, until her thighs burnt, past an arts and crafts store, past burgers and fries, past fish baskets and king salmon stew, past other things she could not afford to try, past rundown video stores and seasonal ice cream parlors. She walked until she heard starving seagulls begging for bread in Sunset Hill Park.

Elevated hundreds of feet, Holly looked down on Puget Sound. It was calm. There was a marina crowded with sailboats. Cars and vans and trucks inched toward what appeared to be a beach further north. The smell of saltwater was on the air. Fifteen feet from her was a bench positioned to take full advantage of the view. Holly walked to it. She allowed a smiling family of four to pass on foot before sitting down. And there she'd sit, for hours, waiting for the gray to dissipate, all to see those westward peaks on the other side, doing what she could to slow her breathing, to shove what had transpired out to sea.

###

The tears came moments after Donald Koh left her apartment, and they weren't alone. Screams came, incoherent screams, violent screams into her air mattress, into the throw pillow she'd bought weeks ago. $300. That's all Donald—wiry, preppy, kind-eyed Donald—had offered after twice insisting it was a plate of Korean origin, not Japanese, after running his fingers along the dings on the backside of the plate, dings Holly had never noticed but could not dispute. $300 because he could hear the tears forming first in her throat. $300 because he saw her as a charity case, yet another thing she could not dispute, a girl unable to attain what she wanted on her own, a girl not to hug but to give money to. Because his $300 would fix it all; it's all he could comprehend as possible. She cried and screamed for that, for being pathetic, for the knots of shame in her stomach. She cried and screamed for the mother she desired but did not know, in intervals, in short bursts, cheeks slipping on the plastic covering of her air mattress.

Half an hour later, Holly was on her side, silent, listening to the elevator in the hallway go up and down. Neighboring doors opened and closed, footsteps back and forth, voices coming and going. She was convinced that she was the only person in Seattle with no place she had to be. Work. A friend's house. A lover's bed. Her family home. Nothing, nowhere.

Yet that was not the catalyst for the second wave of tears. What choked Holly was the reality that she would soon be homeless. Adding Donald's money to her savings, and even depositing the cash she'd withdrawn for the cab driver, still meant that she'd be short on rent. There would surely be a warning before eviction. But a hole was being dug, one from which Holly knew the climb would grow steeper and steeper and steeper. She pictured herself hitchhiking back to Arizona, thumb plugged into the sky, but who would stop? And what would they demand? And what could she trade for those miles but her body—this fucking air mattress? Could she trade her body now, on the street? For $50? For $100? How far could that get her? The only choice she felt like making in this moment, the only thing that made sense, was to cry. And to scream.

For five minutes more, she let it out, more than the first wave, higher, deeper, body coiling like a snake around warmth, gnawing at her pillow, until an incisor punctured the air mattress's casing. Air wheezed out of the hole as she wiggled. Then she cried harder, she screamed louder, and louder, and louder, stopping only when there was one loud knock at her door.

Holly sat up. More air hissed out of the air mattress. She wiped her eyes. And she waited. And she listened. Thirty seconds later, there was another knock, and another, two parts of a rapid series, pop-pop, pop-pop.

"Yeah?" Holly said. Her voice, as congested as it was, cracked.

"My name is Janet LeVitre," came from the other side of the door, high, slightly shrill but muffled. "Are you okay?"

"I'm fine."

"I don't think you are." A moment of silence passed. "My name is Janet LeVitre. I am your neighbor. I live directly above you and I am concerned. I'm not leaving until I see that you're all right." She immediately resumed her knocking, making it abundantly clear that she was not in the business of bluffing. Pop-pop-pop-pop-pop-pop, pop-pop-pop-pop-pop, pop-pop-pop. And on, and on.

When Holly had had enough, she rose and opened the door. And there stood Janet, fortyish and lean, short hair dyed white, large glasses swelling what Holly would notice later were beady eyes. She had braces with alternating green and red bands.

"Thank you," Janet said. She followed Holly into the apartment, conscious not to shut the door behind her, it being her only escape route. Janet took in the studio's emptiness, the bit of gray day allowed in. "Did you just move here?"

Holly plopped onto the air mattress. Air wheezed out. She nodded and sniffled and rubbed her reddening eyes with her fingertips. "From Arizona."

"Very cool," Janet said, "I grew up in Salt Lake City."

Despite wanting someone—anyone—in her life, Holly didn't care. Now, exhausted and embarrassed, was not the time. Here, in this wasteland of a studio, was not the place. She hoped the silence would drive this woman out.

Janet folded her arms and walked around the studio like a mother would, not necessarily judging, but inspecting, poking for fixable blemishes. She looked at the framed photo of young on the floor, in her Yosemite Sam sweatshirt, and smiled. Then at the ceiling, at the water stains. "Holy shit," she said. "If we don't get that fixed, my tub's going to fall next to your bed." She turned to see Holly wipe her eyes. "Look, I don't know what's troubling you, and I don't know if I'd act any different if I were in your shoes, but I want you to know that I'm only here to help. Do you understand?"

"Yes."

"And I can't help if you don't tell me what's wrong. Do you understand that?"

"Yes."

"Can you talk about it?"

"Yes." Holly still couldn't bring herself to look at her for any longer than a glance. In flashes, she watched Janet cross the room, to the air mattress. When she plopped down, a large gust of air burst open the hole Holly had created earlier. The air mattress sank slowly to the floor.

"Ahh," Janet said. "Here I was thinking you couldn't stop farting."

Holly smiled, briefly at first, but soon found herself losing ground. The smile turned into a laugh, the laugh into a giggle, the giggle into tears, the tears into sobs. She was hysterical and she rested her head on Janet's shoulder.

"Oh, honey," Janet said. She wrapped her arm around Holly and pulled her close, the shoulder of her yellow t-shirt dampening gold. An old man carrying a bag of groceries stopped near the doorway and stared at the two of them until Janet waved him off down the hall. "You just talk when you're ready, okay?"

When Holly was ready, she told Janet everything. Sam, her father, her mother, Michelle, employment, Craigslist, Penelope's, everything.

"Giovanni might be able to give you an extension," Janet told Holly.

Holly's words were still punctuated by tears. She'd talked to Giovanni that morning, before Donald Koh stopped by. "He told me it was out of his hands."

"Well, fuck him then," Janet said, shaking her head. "We'll figure it out."

###

"You've reached Steve. Sorry I can't make it to the phone right now but if you leave a message after the beep, I'll get back to you as soon as I can."

Beep.

"Hey Dad," Holly said. She paced Janet's kitchenette in khaki pants and a light blue t-shirt with the tag still on the collar. Dirty baking dishes were piled in the sink. Sepia-toned photos of a small boy in Spider-Man sweatpants hung on the refrigerator door. An old terrier named Roscoe weaved between Holly's steps. "I just wanted to let you know that I'll be starting a new job tomorrow at a shop called Brocker's. It's west of Seattle, on Bainbridge Island." Holly couldn't remember what else she'd been planning to say. In the silence, she leaned down to pet the dog. "Anyway, that's all, really. I hope you're doing okay. Call when you can." She paused then, long enough to feel her stomach turn. "Love you.

After she hung up, Holly walked into the living area. Janet was seated in a rocking chair near the window, needling the first stitches of a pink and blue scarf. "Aren't you glad I made you do that?"

"I guess." Holly was, though. Even if he never called her back, Holly was okay with picturing her father listening to that message, incapable of uncurling a smile.

"Of course you are," Janet said. She set the yarn and needles on the floor, then stood up and slipped on her turquoise windbreaker. "You ready to go?"

"Where?"

"The shop." Janet grabbed a hefty set of keys from the nail they hung on.

"I don't start until tomorrow, do I?"

Janet smiled. Her teeth looked like Christmas. "No, but you need a lay of the land."

###

Aside from the wake of the ferry, Puget Sound was quiet, crisp. The sky was split gray and blue, the sun peeking through in spurts. The ferry continued to pick up speed. The islands—what had appeared from Seattle as gradual mounds of green—grew larger by the second, docked sailboats bobbing in the water, stone houses extending out of those green mounds, their chimneys puffing smoke. Behind it all were the Olympic Mountains, those westward mountains Holly had stared at so often, had longed for. It was calming, she found, the view. Her heartbeat was slower, her face and jaw and neck with as little tension as she could remember them having.

"Sounds like a freak show, right?" Janet said, referring to the shop she owned, a café-slash-trinket-slash-gift-shop-slash-art-gallery. "For the longest time, it moved with me and my ex-husband. St. Louis to Tulsa, Tulsa to Santa Barbara, Santa Barbara to Portland, blah, blah, blah. All over the place. I sold coffee out of cars, paintings out of vans, anything I had, really."

Holly watched tourists on deck snap pictures of one another. Families with selfie sticks. "Was that your maiden name? Brocker?"

Janet joined Holly in leaning on the railing. "Brock was my son's name." As if she knew Holly would have questions, Janet continued without pause, without so much as a blink: "He turned six before he was run over by a semi-truck. Doctors said it had to have been close to painless, something that large squashing something so small, you know?"

Holly pictured it: a summer day, an elevated street, a stray ball, and Brock, cute and blonde and curious, chasing, just chasing that ball. She could feel him go under the tires.

"I'm so sorry, Janet."

Janet smiled. "I know you are, sweetie." She kept her eyes on the various birds circling the ferry, flying in loose formation as if guiding the boat to shore. "But it wasn't anyone's fault. It really wasn't. Brock was clueless, the driver was busy. Things collide, Holly. Things collide and we feel sorry about it, sometimes for years." Janet faced Holly, dry-eyed, comfortable. "Eventually, we grow tired of feeling sorry. And, when we stop, that's when we truly act, that's when we do great things."

"That's when you named it Brocker's."

"It was L & J's before. The L stood for Leon."

"Your husband?" After Janet nodded, Holly asked: "Where is he now?"

"Don't care," Janet said. "Haven't talked to him for years. Even before Brock was killed, he and I were going to shit. He knew it. I knew it." She kept her eyes on the water. "And I was a wreck, Holly. No, seriously. That's the only word for it. Wreck."

Holly pictured a thinner Janet, a hungrier Janet, a sharper Janet, pointed not just at her elbows and wrists, but at her shoulders and hips. A brunette Janet wrapped in a quilt, looking through bedroom blinds at the sunrise.

"When he said he was going to divorce me—God, it was only months after Brock—when he said that, something came over me. Sadness? No. Frustration? No. Just straight to anger." Janet stared at Holly. "I went after him with a meat tenderizer. We lived in West Seattle at the time and in that house we had this great big living room window. And that's where Leon went after he told me he'd be divorcing me. He just walked away from me and kept his back turned. In the kitchen, we had all of our utensils hanging, and I grabbed the thing closest to me. I squeezed that thing tight, and I went after him. But that's all I remember. To this day, that's it." She then inched her windbreaker sleeves to her forearms. "As I inched out of the blackout, the first thing I remember seeing were the handcuffs. The first thing I heard was the dispatcher's voice over the radio—no clue what she said, something riddled with code. And, the first thing I felt? The first thing I felt, believe it or not, was relief. That I was going somewhere. And that someone was taking me there."

Once the initial shock of Janet's story passed through Holly, empathy triumphed. She placed herself as much as she could into Janet's shoes, into that relationship, into that scene, into that trauma, that hell, finding herself amazed at the outcome, at who the person before her had become. Yet, Holly looped again and again around one question, knowing then, understanding the glaring difference between she and Janet:

"Why didn't you leave Seattle?"

At which Janet smiled, and pointed to Bainbridge Island, then back to Seattle. "Brock still lives here." Silence. The circling gulls. "He loved it, Holly. Absolutely loved it. The water, the mountains, the parks, the shops, you name it." What Janet did next—not so much of a nod, but a tilt of her head—allowed an expression in her eyes that declared what she was about to say was perhaps the most honest thing she ever would. "I still live for him."

As she looked at Janet, there was some unexplainable ping in Holly's gut that she took as a message. This, it said, at least for now, is exactly where you are supposed to be.

Holly touched Janet's arm and, though she questioned she could say it with as much certainty as she'd desire, said, "You're a good mother."

\#\#\#

One Space Needle keychain, one Pike Place Market keychain, and two posters of Bob Marley, one in concert, one where he's kicking a soccer ball. After she rang the items into the cash register—her fingers had become like a pianist's: active, spidery, never searching for combinations or rhythm, but knowing exactly where she'd left them—Holly placed all items into one bag and handed it to the mother standing on the other side of the counter. She, like her husband and programmer son, who were horsing around near the exit, wore a black Microsoft cap and a white Xbox t-shirt.

What came next, after the transaction and generic "Thank you, have a great day," had, in three weeks, become Holly's favorite part of the job: the mother would walk to her family, turning around once, and only once, to get another glimpse of Holly. Boldly, she'd then announce in front of all souls in the store that the girl behind the counter was cute, and friendly, and that the son should ask her out. The son's face would turn pink. He'd wipe his sweaty hands on his jeans, and shake his head, the expression on his face one not of rejection, but indecision, and fear, of doing so in public. He'd back his way out of the store, and the mother, the sweet mother would give Holly a look that was both an apology and a promise, that the son would be back. And then, a quick smile and wave from the father, and they'd be gone.

The whole display would make Holly smile. She felt like she was doing everything right—the tasks of her position, the customer service, even her look: the bit of make-up she'd been putting on, the smile, striking enough for both mothers and sons, even if it led to her politely declining. Emerging from the storage room behind the cash register was Greta, carrying a small box of magnets she was to place on the twirling display twenty feet away, near the east wall. Greta was a part-timer who shaved her own head, had piercings from eyebrow to chin, and wore a facial expression that projected only a fifth of the attitude she truly had. Often she refused to wear the uniform, the pink and black argyle polo shirts Janet had chosen because of how hip she (mistakenly) thought they looked. Instead, Greta would show up in long-sleeved t-shirts, sometimes even sweaters, something with enough length to conceal the palm tree tattoos on her wrists—points of embarrassment.

"Saving money to get those fuckers removed," she'd said on Holly's first day.

Greta wasn't someone you tried to steer, uniform code or otherwise, especially if you were Janet. At twenty-six, Greta had been a baker before, she'd been a barista, a cashier, even a custodian. She was a jackknife Janet could place anywhere.

As she set the box on the counter, Greta saw Holly's lingering smile. "Jesus, another one?"

"Another one," Holly said.

"Send him my way next time, would ya? This gal's bed has been far too cold." Greta nudged Holly with her elbow and smiled. She cracked her neck, then looked out past the counter, at the one elderly regular, Mrs. Kroiberg, who was holding a t-shirt to her chest, deciding whether or not the size would fit. "What a slow damn day."

"Slow damn week," Holly said.

"It'll pick up. You just wait—come summer, you'll be wishing for days like this."

Before Holly could respond, jogging across the store was Janet, hand securing the ridiculous baker's cap to her head, flour handprints all over her dark blue shirt. "Girls!" she yelled. "Girls, I'm experimenting!"

"What has gotten into her?" Greta mumbled before Janet reached the counter.

"I need your opinion, girls. I either want to make chocolate chip banana muffins or this Irish coffee recipe I've been meaning to try. I'll make both eventually but what do you want right now?"

Greta: "Chocolate banana."

Holly: "Chocolate banana."

"Chocolate banana it is," Janet said. "We'll make the Irish coffee muffins later," Janet said to Holly, then winked. And, like that, she was off again, jogging through the store.

Greta watched Holly for a moment, noticed a subtle shake of her head. "That wink though?"

"It's nothing," Holly said.

"That shake of your head said it was something," Greta said.

She had to tell her. If she didn't, Janet would. Later today, tomorrow, next week, sometime soon it would surface. "Last night, Janet asked me to move in with her," Holly said. Over tomato basil penne and merlot, she had. She'd said that Seattle was expensive, that she saw Holly as a daughter, that they were basically roommates already and that little would change if they searched for an apartment together, a loft out of Giovanni Brenko's grasp.

"Are you going to?" Holly had expected a cackle rivaling a hyena's, but Greta asked this sincerely.

"I told her I'd think about it."

Greta nodded, then picked up the box of magnets. "I think you should." Before she walked around the counter and to the twirling display, she added, "If you don't, fuck it, I will. How could you not love that woman over there?"

And Greta was right. How could she not? If it weren't for Janet, Holly would be on the street, or back in Arizona. And Janet was still saving her: Janet had for a month of Holly's rent, for all of Holly's new clothes, for all of Holly's public transit fare. Janet took Holly grocery shopping, then made Holly's meals. Bought her shampoo and conditioner, makeup and nail polish. They'd gone to movies, they'd grabbed coffee, they'd seen Alonzo Bodden together at Parlor Live. "At least until you're on your feet," she'd said to Holly, slipping the doorman a $20 bill to bypass their assigned seating for the front row, something she claimed was because she hoped the two of them would be ribbed by Alonzo himself.

Tender. Thoughtful. Generous. Three words Holly knew she'd use to describe Janet if asked, but three words that, though she couldn't fully comprehend why, had begun to instill within Holly a fear she'd never known: that she was being had. That Janet's charity was not a product of altruism, but perhaps a series of selfish acts with one goal: to redistribute the weight of the son she'd buried, to set it upon Holly, her new brace.

Recalling the condition Janet had found her in, Holly began to blame her worry on the speed of it all, on she and Janet's trajectory, on the fact that she herself could not accept without hesitation what she'd desired for so long—something good, something wholesome. This shouldn't be happening to me, Holly had thought, time and time again since meeting Janet. I don't deserve good things.

Holly looked at Janet then, in the café portion of the store. Watched her toss a small ball of dough at Frank, a distant cousin of hers she'd flown in from Lyon after seeing on his Instagram stories just how skilled he was with desserts. She laughed. She returned to mixing something in a large glass bowl. She couldn't stop smiling.

I have to move in with her, Holly thought then. I owe her that much. I have to.

"Excuse me, miss?" It was Mrs. Kroiberg. She was at the counter, looking every bit of seventy-three and wafting a lilac scent as she walked. Once she saw Holly was out of her daze, she held up a gray and orange t-shirt that said, DON'T !^&* WITH SEATTLE. "Do you have any mediums back there?"

"Let me check for you, Mrs. Kroiberg," Holly said, then went into the storage room. There were boxes stacked on the floor—more magnets, more keychains, more Christmas ornaments, puzzles and board games. Above the boxes was a clothes rack whose center was bowing, sweaters and jackets shoved to the sides to compensate. Holly flipped through the t-shirts, checking tags, finding a medium DON'T !^&* WITH SEATTLE. "I found it, Mrs. Kroiberg," Holly announced. But, when she walked through the storage room doorway, it was not Mrs. Kroiberg she saw.

At the counter was an Asian woman wearing gray business slacks and a collared purple top. If it weren't for the few wrinkles around her eyes, Holly would've guessed she was in her early thirties. Her black hair was in a ponytail, an unsure smile pulled across her lips and cheeks. There was a scar above her right eyebrow.

"Hi Holly," Kaori said. Her voice was low and dense but smoother than Holly had imagined. Velvety.

Still in the doorway, Holly felt her stomach rise, then fall, then rise again. Her mouth went dry. She could not blink.

Mrs. Kroiberg, who had yet to move, slowly merged into Holly's line of sight. "Were you able to find a medium, dear?" She held out her hand as if expecting it to be met with the shirt. "Can I see it, at least?"

Greta, understanding that something was off about the situation, put the box of magnets in her hands down and hurried over to the counter. "I can help you, Mrs. Kroiberg." She stared at Holly before and after taking the t-shirt from her hand. "Everything okay?"

Holly blinked. Holly nodded. There were no tears but she wiped her eyes anyway. Her mother smiled at that. "Hi," Holly finally said, stepping toward the counter. She wasn't sure what came next—What are you doing here? How can I help you?

Kaori stepped closer to the counter, spoke lower. "Your father said I could find you here." When she saw how confused the statement made Holly, she pulled one piece of folded paper from the black purse she kept on her shoulder. "He said you've been in the city since January."

Holly nodded, then took the letter from her mother. Her father's tiny, jagged handwriting was all across the page.

"He also said it was his fault you haven't been able to get a hold of me." Kaori cleared her throat. "Of course he didn't feel that an apology was in order but—but that isn't important. What is important is that you have my information." She set a different slip of paper on the counter, one with her address and phone number, then shook her head. "I know you're at work; I don't expect you to drop everything and come with me right now. That'd be incredibly unfair of me. But, I'd love it if we could get together, have dinner, grab tea, catch up. Whatever you'd like."

Holly, still numb, looked from her father's letter to her mother's eyes, from her mother's eyes to the letter. She looked at Greta, at Greta talking to Mrs. Kroiberg, from Mrs. Kroiberg to Pierre and, finally, to Janet, who had taken off her baker's cap, who now stared at Holly in confusion, wondering if it was an unruly customer Holly was dealing with, someone needing to speak with the owner, someone needing to be straightened out by overwhelming kindness.

"Holly?" Kaori waited for Holly's attention, then said: "How does that sound?"

Holly folded the letter. Hand it back to her. She did. Move your feet. Smile. "That sounds good," she said, surprised at how composed her own voice was, how strong, how impenetrable. "I'll call you when my shift is over."

Kaori smiled. She placed the letter back into her purse, slung the purse back over her shoulder and, before walking toward the exit, said: "I look forward to it."

Holly then took her mother's information from the counter and stuffed it into her pants pocket. She took in her surroundings: Greta still chatted with Mrs. Kroiberg; Pierre worked some dough; Janet was on her way over.

She'd ask Holly who that was, what the woman wanted, and Holly would say, "That was my mother," and Janet would nod, and maybe she would wink, and Holly would smile, all afternoon she would smile and, when her shift was over, when another day was done at Brocker's, she'd punch out and, while walking to the ferry with Janet, she'd call her father. She'd call her mother. Then, she'd go home.

DEAR HOLLY, BE RIGHT

a *Strays Like Us* story by Garrett Francis

ABOUT THE AUTHOR

Garrett Francis is the author of the novel *And in the Dark They Are Born* and the short story collection *Strays Like Us*. He grew up on a small farm in Michigan and earned his B.A. in Creative Writing from Grand Valley State University.

In 2012, Garrett co-founded *Squalorly*, a digital literary journal of the Midwest and served as its nonfiction editor until 2014.

In 2016, founded Orson's Publishing in 2016, a micro press and served as the press's sole editor (and designer, and publicist, among other roles) until its closure in 2020, publishing four book-length works by new and emerging authors.

He also founded *Orson's Review* in 2017, a digital literary journal that served as a companion to its parent press, publishing fiction, creative nonfiction, poetry and photography. He served as the sole editor of *Orson's Review* as well, and is proud to have helped bring the work of over 70 international contributors to life.

Today, Garrett lives in the Pacific Northwest with his family. Short works of his have been published in literary journals like

Midwestern Gothic, Barely South Review, Whiskeypaper and *Monkeybicycle.*

Visit authorgarrettfrancis.com to learn more about Garrett and his work.

ISBN: 978-0-9914463-6-0

Published by 5626 Press

9 780991 446360